To Josie, Jack, Addy, and Cooper (and for your **mom** of course!)
~With Love, Julia

TABLE TALK

A book about table manners

Written by JULIA COOK   Illustrated by ANITA DuFALLA

BOYS TOWN
Press

Boys Town, Nebraska

Table Talk

Text and Illustrations Copyright © 2016 by Father Flanagan's Boys' Home
ISBN 978-1-934490-97-6

Published by the Boys Town Press
14100 Crawford St.
Boys Town, NE 68010

For a Boys Town Press catalog, call **1-800-282-6657**
or visit our website: **BoysTownPress.org**

Publisher's Cataloging-in-Publication Data

Names: Cook, Julia, 1964- author. | DuFalla, Anita, illustrator.

Title: Table talk : a book about table manners / written by Julia Cook ; illustrated by Anita DuFalla.

Other titles: Series: Cook, Julia, 1964- Building relationships ; no. 7.

Description: Boys Town, NE : Boys Town Press, [2016] | Series: Building relationships. | Summary: Written from the table's point of view, this clever tale helps kids understand that table manners include not only table etiquette, but also being respectful, kind, and considerate to others.--Publisher.

Identifiers: ISBN: 978-1-934490-97-6

Subjects: LCSH: Table etiquette--Juvenile fiction. | Etiquette for children and teenagers--Juvenile fiction. | Courtesy--Juvenile fiction. | Respect--Juvenile fiction. | Thoughtfulness--Juvenile fiction. | Children--Life skills guides--Juvenile fiction. | Interpersonal relations in children--Juvenile fiction. | CYAC: Table etiquette--Fiction. | Etiquette--Fiction. | Respect--Fiction. | Thoughtfulness--Fiction. | Conduct of life--Fiction. | Interpersonal relations--Fiction.

Classification: LCC: PZ7.C76984 T33 2016 | DDC: [E]--dc23

Printed in the United States
10 9 8 7 6 5 4 3 2

Boys Town Press is the publishing division of Boys Town, a national organization serving children and families.

I am "The Table," so sit up close to me. And listen to my "TABLE TALK." I'll tell you how to be!

Having good table manners is a must,
if you want to be your best.
I'll tell you what you need to know,
and I'll show you all the rest.

Did you know that table manners really matter?
They're more than just about eating.
They're about being kind and considerate of others,
and being respectful of people's feelings.

You may be **cute, important,** and **smart,**
but know this for a fact...
If you have bad table manners, people will notice,
and judge you by the way you act.

Make sure your face and hands are clean before you sit down by me. I don't want to be the place where germs get spread!
I want to be
GERM-FREE!!!!

Being a table makes me lucky.
I get to be the place
where people come together,
and enjoy talking "face-to-face."

Don't talk on your phone or text at the table.
I've been waiting here all day.
I can't wait for you to sit by me.
I *want* to hear what YOU have to say!

Mealtime is very special.
You get to spend TIME with others.
If your face is buried in a video game,
you can't talk to one another.

Please leave your video games in your room.
Or put them right in here!
People forgetting to talk to each other...
is one of my greatest fears!

Devices in basket
during mealtime

When you sit in your chair,
don't hunch way down

or **lean**

way over your plate.

Rest your forearms
(not your elbows) on the table.
And do your best to *sit up straight.*

If your mealtime is not a buffet,
you sure don't want to be *rude*.
Before you sit down and start to eat,
wait 'til everyone has their food.

13

When someone puts food on your plate,
say **"Thank you"** and give it a try.
If you say something like

"That looks yucky!"

You might just make the cook **cry**.

If the food tastes **nasty,** spit it out in a napkin while you pretend to wipe your face. Spitting out food in front of others will cause a **BIG disgrace!**

15

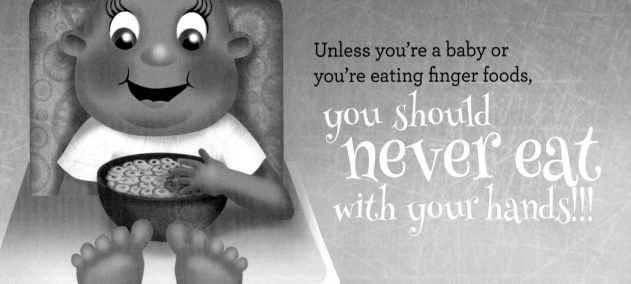

And please use your fork
to pick up your food,
or your spoon whenever you can.

Unless you're a baby or
you're eating finger foods,

you should
never eat
with your hands!!!

Don't stuff your mouth full of food,
or take too big of a bite.
It looks **gross** and
you might **choke.**

This bite looks
about right.

If you try to talk when your mouth **IS FULL**,
you'll make a big mistake.
People can't understand what you are saying,
and you might spray someone with cake!!!

And I don't want to hear you eat either.
So please don't smack your lips,
or **grunt** or *hum* while you chew your food.
People don't like that one bit!!!

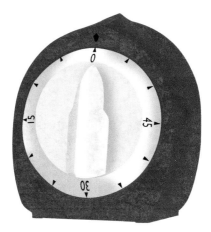

Eat slowly,
DON'T GOBBLE,
ENJOY YOUR FOOD.

Your meal took time to prepare.
Wait five seconds between each bite,
and show the cook how much you care.

If you see something you want on the table,
don't reach over somebody's plate.

Ask for that item
to be passed to you.
It won't be that long of a wait.

Don't use your sleeve to wipe off your mouth. Use your napkin for that instead.

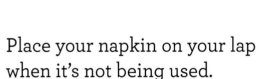

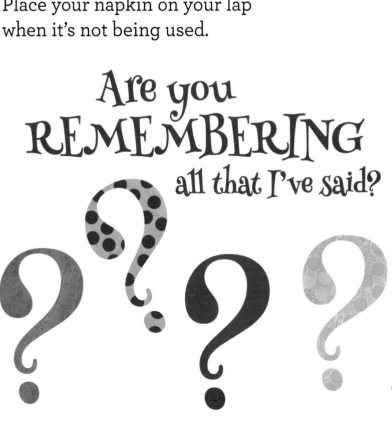

Place your napkin on your lap when it's not being used.

Are you
REMEMBERING
all that I've said?

23

Never blow your nose with your napkin,
or wipe off your entire face.
Excuse yourself and go to the restroom,
and do that in the right place.

24

Whenever you drink at the table,
you must try hard not to SLURP.
And excuse yourself quickly if you have gas,
because it's rude to toot and burp!!!!

If a gas bubble slips out on accident,
make sure you say, "Excuse me!"
Gas bubbles at times can be very tricky.
Don't you all agree?

Always **thank the cook** when you are done eating, and *ask to be excused.*
You'll find that mealtime is a lot more fun, when you act the way you should.

I am "The Table" and I know this stuff!!!

These things I know for sure.
*Using good table manners is a **MUST**,*
if you want to do well in this world!

I know there's lots to remember,
so let me tell you what I've found.
You'll need to practice and be reminded a ton,
before you will have it all down.

So the next time you go to sit down
at a table that's just like me,
remember my TABLE TALK and...

be the BEST you,
you can be!!!

30

Teaching Kids Good Table Manners

Good table manners are learned social skills that help children (and adults) navigate the world more effectively. When a person has good table manners, he or she demonstrates an understanding of being kind, considerate, and respectful of others. People who use poor table manners are often critically judged by those around them, which can lead to character flaw assumptions.

Here is a list of table manners to remember and apply.

- Make sure your face and hands are clean before sitting down at the table.

- Do not bring cell phones, tablets, computers, and/or video games to the table at mealtime. This is a great place to practice talking to one another face-to-face.

- Sit up straight. Try to avoid hunching way down in your chair or leaning way over your plate.

- Don't talk when there is food in your mouth.

- When someone puts food on your plate, say "Thank you" and give it a try.

- If you don't like the food, and you need to spit it out, place your napkin over your mouth and spit it out into your napkin. Never spit food back onto your plate.

- Always use utensils to pick up your food unless you are eating finger foods (hamburgers, fries, pizza, etc.). It's not polite to eat with your hands.

- Don't take too big of a bite or stuff your mouth full of food.

- Don't start eating until everyone has food on their plates.

- Don't hum, smack your lips, or make other noises while you are eating.

- If you see something you want on the table, politely ask someone to pass it to you. Don't reach across somebody's plate to get it. And always remember to say "Please" and "Thank you."

- Never blow your nose into your napkin. Instead, excuse yourself and go to the restroom and use a tissue.

- Never use your sleeve to wipe off your face. Use your napkin.

- Try hard not to pass gas at the table. If you accidentally do, always say "Excuse me."

- Wait at least 5 seconds between each bite – don't gobble.

- Thank the cook when you are finished eating.

- Always ask to be excused.

- Push in your chair when you leave the table.

- Close your mouth when you chew your food.

Say YES to Good Manners!

For more parenting information, visit boystown.org/parenting.

BOYS TOWN® Parenting

Boys Town Press Books
by Julia Cook

Kid-friendly books to teach social skills

978-1-944882-05-1

978-1-934490-97-6

978-1-934490-30-3

978-1-934490-39-6

978-1-934490-47-1

978-1-934490-48-8

978-1-934490-62-4

978-1-934490-86-0

Reinforce the social skills RJ learns in each book.*

BEST ME I Can Be!

978-1-934490-43-3

978-1-934490-49-5

978-1-934490-67-9

Other Titles: *The Worst Day of My Life Ever!, I Just Don't Like the Sound of NO!, Sorry, I Forgot to Ask!* and *Teamwork Isn't My Thing and I Don't Like to Share!*

*Accompanying posters sets and activity guides are available.

COMMUNICATE with Confidence

Help kids master the art of communicating.

978-1-944882-13-6

978-1-934490-58-7

Other Titles: *Well, I Can Top That!* and *Gas Happens!*

978-1-944882-08-2

Responsible ME!

978-1-934490-80-8

978-1-944882-09-9

Other Titles:
That Rule Doesn't Apply to Me! and *Baditude!*

BoysTownPress.org

For information on Boys Town, its Education Model®, Common Sense Parenting®, and training programs:
boystowntraining.org | boystown.org/parenting
training@BoysTown.org | 1-800-545-5771

For parenting and educational books and other resources:
BoysTownPress.org
btpress@BoysTown.org | 1-800-282-6657